Mary Edwards Pater

DRAGONS OF DOGGERLAND

Mary Edwards-Porter

Illustrated by Megan Dobbyn

Published by BonnyBooks

DRAGONS OF DOGGERLAND

First published in the UK in 2022 by BonnyBooks
mary-edwards-porter.co.uk

ISBN 978-1-3999-2902-8

Printed and bound in Great Britain by
Clays Ltd, Elcograf S.p.A.

For Lynda

FROM THE AUTHOR
Mary Edwards-Porter

I don't think I have ever really grown up!

At least, I've never grown out of children's books. I just love them. A chance to lose myself in another world and, perhaps discover new things, people, and other creatures. When you read something, it is all in your own head and your own imagination.

This is why I have written about Doggerland. As soon as I heard about it, I was captivated. A secret world that is now under the sea! It remained hidden for thousands of years, but slowly people began to realise that this flooded land had been home to people and wildlife living out their own adventures, a very long time ago.

It's funny that nobody has ever mentioned the Dogger dragons before, so I wanted to make sure their story was told. One of my readers said: "Most dragons in stories are fierce. Yours are kind. And why don't they have scales and wings like other dragons?" I said she would have to wait until Book Three for the answer to that. I haven't finished writing it yet, but I know how it ends.

mary-edwards-porter.co.uk

N
E
W
S

THE BIG WAVE

SEAHORSES' HOME

OLD VOLCANO

SHALLOW LANDS AND MARSHES

10

DOGGERLAND

DOGGER BANK HILL

DRAGONS' DEN

BIG LAKE

SHALLOW LANDS AND MARSHES

BERRY'S HOME

WOLF LAKE

Dogger dragons aren't fierce. They are friendly and kind.

They don't have scales and wings like most dragons but are smooth-skinned and smooth-natured.

They can look a bit alarming when they speak, as words come rushing out in a wave of steam.

They don't speak English! I have translated as near as I can what they were saying to each other and to those other beings who understood them. If you or I had actually been there, what we would have heard would have probably sounded a bit like a series of sighs, snorts, squeaks, and sort of "shishing" noises!

THE DRAGON FAMILY

LONGTAIL

Goldflame's
daughter. Lazy,
but she has a
lovely long tail!

GOLDFLAME

Mother dragon,
lost without
her husband
Steamer.

STEAMER

Long lost father.

WHISTLER

Long lost baby
brother.

FIRECREST

The oldest son. He gets
into trouble too much
and spends a lot of
time on his own.

IN DOGGERLAND
AROUND 7500 YEARS AGO

Doggerland was a real place and was home to all sorts of animals and plants, including human beings.

It used to be land, joining what is nowadays England, to the Netherlands and Denmark, but is now under the North Sea.

WHERE ARE WE NOW

There is a boy, with long dark hair and wearing
an old boar-skin tunic. He is hanging on to the
tail of a large green, panicking dragon. There
is a hairy black dog hanging on to his belt with
gritted teeth. All three are being swept along by
a tidal wave of mega proportions and at such a

speed and a roaring of water that you'd never see anything like it if you lived to be a hundred.

The boy is shouting and screaming but it's impossible to hear what he is saying. The dragon is staring ahead, concentrating hard on not getting slammed into anything, as massive tree trunks are being swept along beside them. The dog would like to bark but if he does, he might lose his grip, so he keeps his (terrified) thoughts to himself. The giant wave is propelling them from the sea inland threatening to slam them against trees and rocks as they speed along. The shoreline and its standing trees are fast approaching... As the boy goes by, at last we can hear him:

"TURN ON THE STEAM!" he screams at the dragon. The dragons face turns from terrified to excited. Eyes shining, he takes a deep breath and "WHOOOOSH!"

Like a rocket motor he blasts out a stream of steam against the oncoming wall of tree trunks. They bend away from him, but it is enough to break their speed as the waves rush past them and they crash against the broken up remains of branches and tree trunks.

All three lie stunned on the ground of what used to be the edge of a wood, but now looks more like a wrecked beach. The thundering wall of water rumbles on into the distance. Shrieking birds and howling animals can be heard as the waves wreak havoc inland.

The dog finally lets go of the belt and takes in a deep breath. He is panting now but at least he can breathe. The dragon sits up, looking stunned, snorting steam from his frightened nostrils. The boy looks soaked to the skin and asleep. The dog licks his face to try and wake him, but he doesn't stir. After the rushing of the waves has gone, there is now almost silence. No bird song or movement from any other animals. Just the sounds of a snorting dragon and a black dog licking a young boy's face, hoping he can get him to wake up.

CHAPTER ONE

BEFORE iT HAPPENED

Everyone loved the Dogger dragons. Massive, long, gentle and green, with wavy crests on their backs and green or gold spots, they would float lazily in the lush swampy still waters of the flat plains of Doggerland.

Nobody had a bad word to say against them. It wasn't because the dragons were kind, (which they were). It wasn't because they never picked fights, (which they didn't). It was more because of what they ate which pleased everybody.

There was nothing a Dogger dragon liked

more, than a mouthful of mosquitoes. Any little flies would do, but they particularly liked the buzzy, biting or stinging flies, like midges or gnats. The taste has "more bite" as the "Dragon Big Book of Tasty Meals", puts it.

In the calm lakes of Doggerland, if it got a bit peckish, all a dragon had to do was float about on the surface, perhaps thinking great thoughts, perhaps singing a dragon song, or perhaps more or less asleep. When it heard the whine of mosquitoes, it might open a lazy eye to check, take a deep breath, then "Whoosh!" out of its nostrils would come a long sheet of flame. Down would come the frazzled mosquitoes, into the waiting wide open mouth of the dragon. It took a lot of flies to fill up a Dogger dragon, but thankfully there were plenty of flies about, as they bred in the lake and there was always plenty of water.

A Dogger dragon can turn down the heat and send steam out of its nostrils instead of flames. It can cook a meal more gently or it can make steam-messages to send to other dragons.

There is nothing a young dragon likes more than to play "dragon zoomies", shooting around on the surface very fast indeed, but by nature of the nostrils being at the front, this means it all happens BACKWARDS. For a few, mad minutes, chaos results, and other animals have to get out of the way, until either there is a big

crash, or the dragon gets TOLD OFF and has to
COME IN AT ONCE

It was amongst this happy scene that there lived
a boy. With dark shaggy hair, nut-brown skin and
a leather tunic, he looked as if he had grown out
of the undergrowth around him. He had a belt
around his waist, a bag over his shoulders and a
bracelet of small pink and brown cowrie shells
around one wrist. The bracelet was his lucky
charm, made for him, long ago, by his mother,
who he could now scarcely remember.

He couldn't remember his real name either,

but we can call him Berry as that is what the dragons called him. You'll find out why in a minute.

Berry had lived all his (quite short) life beside the lake, which was called the BIG LAKE (people in those days didn't have time for a lot of imagination). When he was very young, he used to watch the grown-ups hunting and gathering food. Sometimes they caught fish and sometimes they hunted wild boar. Sometimes they collected seeds and berries. Berry used to be good at collecting berries – the dragons used to watch him, so you can see now how he got his name! Blackberries were his favourite fruit, and he had learnt to avoid those berries that made him sick. He was a fisherman now too and had built his own boat out of a dug-out tree trunk, and a landing stage from tree poles he had cut down and lashed together with rope made from creepers.

As he had no one except himself to look after (not counting Growler, who looked after himself, and sometimes had to look after Berry too, as we shall see), it didn't take him long to catch enough fish for him to eat.

The Others had disappeared after a huge storm one night when Berry was quite little. He remembers his mother shouting and he remembers crying out, but he had been washed out to sea, clinging to a floating log. If it hadn't been for a passing dragon spotting him many days later, he would have surely died. By the time he had made his way back, through fallen tree trunks and mess, the Others had gone, and their homes had been destroyed. He searched and called for a while, but all he found was Growler.

Growler couldn't tell him where he had come from, but he was obviously lost as well, so, they had stuck together ever since.

The dragons had found their way back to the lake too, but there were less of them, and they looked quiet and sad, not like their usual snorting and steaming selves.

Berry was happy. There were still more storms and bad weather than there used to be, and the sea and the lake water seemed to be getting higher, but he had plenty to eat and had made a cosy little shelter to live in. He had Growler for company and to guard him, and the dragons… well the dragons were always there, snorting, zooming, spraying, making waves, and, most importantly, eating up all the biting insects!

Berry loved the dragons. He had learnt to understand their snorts and squeaks and they seemed to understand him. They made him laugh. He had tried to swim with them a couple of times, but if one of them suddenly decided to play "backwards zoomies" it would all happen so fast that he couldn't get out of the way quickly enough, so it was a bit risky! He had caught

Growler once or twice riding on the back of

a dragon called Firecrest, his ears flapping in

FIRECREST

the wind and eyes bright with delight. He told

him off as he thought it was too dangerous, but

Growler just gave him one of those "I'm just a

dog so I don't understand" looks, and only did it again once, well... perhaps more than once...

Growler's dragon friend Firecrest was ALWAYS getting into trouble. The only dragon who had ever been able to get through to him was his father, Steamer. Steamer had been big, handsome, and kind and Firecrest had adored him. But since the night that Whistler, his baby brother, had got lost in a big storm, and Steamer had gone out into the dark to look for him, and neither of them had ever come home, the family had been devastated.

Firecrest's mother, Goldflame had called and called night and day and Firecrest had never been the same. He spent many hours on his own. Sometimes he found Growler and the two of them just mucked about in the water for a bit, and other times he had swum the long, difficult swim down to the sea. Amongst the wonderful underwater forests of seaweed, he had discovered his little pink friends – the seahorses. They were TINY, but Firecrest used to watch them play in the waving seaweed fronds. He found them fascinating, and, somehow, they reminded him of his little brother Whistler.

That's where he was this morning, lazily swimming and bobbing about, every now and then turning over to pop his face underwater and watch his little seahorse friends.

CHAPTER TWO

IT ALL CHANGES

The morning had started with Goldflame telling Longtail and Firecrest that they needed to stay in the den and help her clean it out, ready to put cosy new bedding in for the winter. To Firecrest and Longtail this all sounded a bit too much like WORK.

Firecrest said something about having an important date to meet up with his seahorse friends and he was suddenly gone.

Longtail swished her beautiful long tail about, as if to brush up some dirty twigs, but somehow had found herself outside, and then, by some miracle, she was by the lake, on the sunny edge, and then floating about lazily on her back in the warm shallow water.

"Where have you both gone?" asked Goldflame to the empty air in the empty den.

"Just me then" smiled Goldflame to herself knowing that if they didn't want to help, she was probably best doing it herself anyway. She looked out of the den entrance, watching Longtail dreamily bobbing about on the water. She wondered, not for the first time, how on Earth she was going to keep her family together without her adored husband Steamer.

On the other side of the lake, Berry had decided that he fancied a change. He knew that at this time of the year he could scrape limpets off the rocks on the beach, catch sea fish, crabs, and shrimps. He knew which seaweeds he could eat. Yes, it was just a perfect day to go down to the sea!

Growler knew from the nets and carved wooden pots Berry was packing, that this was going to be a beach trip. He started to wag his tail and jump up and down. "GRRREAT!" he growled, bounding around Berry as if that were helping. Together, they took everything down to the landing stage. Growler carried the tied-up leather pouch which contained Berry's pack-up lunch of dried fish, berries, and flat bread, as well as Growler's favourite old deer antler. Soon everything was loaded into the dug-out canoe. Growler leapt in, rocking the boat just as Berry was reaching for his wooden oar, and nearly tipped them both in the water. "Whoa!" shouted

Berry and laughed. The sun was making the water surface sparkle, and it was a warm day. He wasn't in the mood to get cross. He pushed off with the oar, turned the boat around, and headed off to the end of the lake, to follow the river to the sea.

Growler lay at the front of the boat, hairy chin resting on the prow, ears up, eyes shining, excitedly looking out for anything new. The waters got a bit choppy as the river current met the sea, and he had to grip on with his furry black paws as Berry struggled to row them out further. Suddenly, Growler sat up with excitement "WOOF!" (He didn't have a very wide range of words). In the distance he could see the large, lonely shape of his friend Firecrest, gently swimming around, every now and then turning on his tummy, to watch the waters underneath him. "WOOF!" (Again... I told you...). Growler leapt into the water and swam a very impressive doggy paddle out towards his huge friend.

Firecrest rolled lazily on to his back, then turned and spotted Growler:

"SNORT!" he blew, excitedly, seeing his little furry friend. With a swish of his massive tail, he was alongside Growler in seconds, and with a (slightly embarrassing) scrabbling of paws and a bit of splashing, Growler was on his back. With only a slight backwards glance at Berry, they were off, out to sea, playing and laughing in a sort of doggy-dragon way.

Berry opened his mouth to call Growler back, but he could see how much fun he was having. To be honest, he could probably hunt for fish and crabs much better on his own. He stood up carefully, swaying from side to side with the rolling current of the sea, and bent down to unfurl his fishing net. He had made it himself from plant fibres, tree bark (for floats) and stones (for the weights) and it worked well. There were so many fish in the sea, he only had to lower it for a few minutes, leave it dragging behind his little boat, and he would have enough fresh fish to last a few days. If he spent longer fishing, he could dry and smoke the fish over a fire, and it would keep for ages. Once the tide had gone out, he would get out of the boat and collect as many limpets and other shellfish and crabs as he could. It was going to be a lovely day!

As he leant over the side as normal, the sea seemed to roll and rush up to meet him. It hit him in the face with such force he fell backwards into the boat. "WHAT???" he shouted. He was struggling back onto his knees and gripping the side of the boat when another wave hit him. Just as he was wondering what was going on (there had been no sign of a storm) he heard a frantic mix of barking and roaring. He looked up. Coming towards him, perched on the top of a roaring wave as high as a tree and as wide as a

wave they had ever seen. It was taking them way past anywhere that they knew. On and on it roared and rolled. As they finally rocketed towards the beach, they could see the sand, rocks and trees which seemed to be rushing towards them. The sea crashed in front of them, shattering and flattening anything it met. They would be smashed into the trees!

"TURN ON THE STEAM!" shouted Berry.

And so, here we are, where we started.

Here's what happened next...

CHAPTER THREE

JOURNEYS

Growler was beginning to think that his human was not going to wake up. Berry was cold and wet to the touch and very still. He looked very pale. He didn't smell right. Growler started to whine. Firecrest gently sniffed with his huge nose. "He needs warming up" he snorted. "Stand back!" Firecrest let out a sheet of flame, aimed at a fallen tree that was lying nearby. Whoosh! it went up in flames. It burnt so well, Growler had to tug on Berry's tunic and pull him back a bit, away from the fire.

Growler licked Berry, ever-so-gently on his forehead and face. Berry groaned, then yawned, then lifted his arm up to wipe at his face. His head felt cut and bruised and sore. His hand felt the familiar nose of a hairy dog. He opened his eyes. "Hello Growler" he mumbled. "WOOF!" said Growler, leaping about and wagging his tail. Firecrest looked on, very pleased with himself.

Berry stretched out, still lying down amongst shattered branches with the sand sticking to his wet skin. He gingerly felt down his legs and up his arms, almost afraid in case he was badly hurt. His fingers touched his lucky bracelet. It was still there! Amazingly, so was his belt, and fastened onto it, his knife and leather pouch with their pack-up lunch!

He dragged himself onto his knees and gave Growler a big hug "Thank you, thank you" he gasped, "Woofle woofle" mumbled Growler, from somewhere inside the hug. Berry turned to Firecrest, who was sitting tall beside them, looking relieved. "THANK YOU," said Berry.

"Ffutt – no problem!" steamed Firecrest.

"We'd better find out where we are," said Berry, standing up carefully as he still felt a bit dizzy. Perhaps he got up too soon as he stumbled over a branch and fell back down. Stretching out to break his fall, his hand grasped at something small and bumpy mixed up with the mess of sand and twigs on the ground. He opened his fist to reveal a bundle of small pink cowrie shells threaded through with gut string, like a necklace. "That's funny. I thought it hadn't broken." His hand automatically went to his wrist. His bracelet. Yes, it was still there. "What?" Stunned, he turned this new string of shells around in his hand, running his fingers along them just to check they were real. Just like his mother used to make! How can this be possible? His mind raced. But it had been YEARS since he had seen any of the Others, so long he thought they had disappeared forever. Yet, here he was, washed up miles from home, holding a necklace, so like his own bracelet.

For years he had thought he was the only one left. For years it hadn't mattered. But THIS! Growler sniffed at him and sniffed at the necklace. This seemed to be important to his human, but he couldn't see why. The shells smelt a bit like fish-food, but they were empty and useless. Brushing the necklace down, Berry put it over his head and around his neck and said: "I'm too tired and hungry to work this out now. I'll get some of this brushwood, build up the fire, make a shelter and settle down for the night while I plan what to do. Oh, and first, we'd better eat something." Growler almost fell onto his antler in hunger. Berry chewed at his dried fish, deep in thought, but making sure that Growler got some of the fish too, as there's not really any meat on an old antler.

Firecrest lifted his great head, looking back towards the retreated waves, the sea, and, somewhere, a long way away, his home den. He let out a deep sigh. Lumbering back to where there was mud and debris and clouds of flies, he busied himself, steaming away at them, trying to get at least half a tummy full. He sighed again, and kept looking up, sniffing the air.

It didn't take long for Berry to make a shelter, there were so many branches around. He and Growler hugged together inside it, while Firecrest lay nearby, a large comforting dome-shape outlined in the pinky-grey sky as the sun set.

It seemed like only five minutes since Berry had dropped off to sleep, but suddenly Growler was sitting up, tense, and shaking, sniffing the air.

"AWOOOOOL!!" Wolf howls! Berry froze. "We must keep very, very still" he whispered, holding Growler tight. Firecrest opened one eye. Dragons were deep sleepers, and they didn't like to be disturbed. Besides which wolves didn't bother them.

But Growler lifted up his chin, pointing his nose to the sky: "AWOOOOOL!" he responded. "Shhh! What are you doing?" Berry was horrified. Growler sat still, listening. "Awoooool!" came the reply. Growler barked some short, gruff barks. There were barks back, which seemed to be getting further away, and then, silence. Berry felt for his friend's lovely, thick fur and stroked him on his forehead. "What was THAT about? Have they really gone?" Growler licked his hand gently and gazed sadly into the dark. The wolves had not been hunting. At least not hunting them. It was a small pack and they had lost a cub in the flood. They had been searching for it all day, but all the water had washed away any trace of scent, and the wolves were losing hope.

Berry tried to settle down to get more sleep, and Firecrest was soon snoring, but Growler sat upright for a very long time, sniffing the air, wondering, if he had puppies, what it would feel like to lose one. He eventually let out a long sigh and settled back down next to Berry. Even though he was very tired he really didn't get much sleep after that.

Morning came suddenly. Berry had slept well in the end. He woke, rubbing his head which was still a bit sore, to find that both friends had been busy in the early hours while he was still snoozing.

"Humph!" declared Growler as he dropped a newly killed fish in front of him. He was licking his lips. It had been so easy! He had found a stream nearby which looked like most of its water had been sucked dry, leaving fish floundering in the mud. He had eaten so many already it seemed only fair to bring some back for Berry. "Well done, Growler!" Growler shot away to get more. He had watched Berry dry fish in the past for storing and he knew the food would come in handy later.

Firecrest had also had his breakfast and had gone some distance away, still in view, but back to the water where he felt more at home and where he could catch little sea-shrimps to add to the fly meal.

It took Berry all morning to cook and wrap the fish in leaves and cram it all in his leather pouch. All the time his mind was racing. Should he try and find his way back home? It shouldn't be too difficult to track his way back. Or should he look for more clues to find who had dropped the necklace? Could it be the Others? His family? His mother?

He looked at Firecrest. Berry knew he was thinking of family too. If Firecrest went back his own way he would lose his big friend, but also an easy way to make fire. Berry had no fire-flints with him and although he could still manage it, it would take more time.

He showed Growler the necklace again. "Growler! Hunt! Hunt!" Nose down, Growler started sniffing and snorting along the ground, looking for traces of "necklace people". Berry walked up and down this new shoreline, on the edge of the broken woods, looking for signs. Perhaps a track or trail? Even an animal track would be good. It wasn't long before Growler was alongside the stream again where he had found the fish. Berry followed. Yes, there was a track! No foot or paw-prints, except for Growler's, as there were too many leaves and branches on the ground, but a definite path of some sort. He looked at the sky. The track was going west, the opposite of home. He wasn't sure how far the wave had taken them, but it would surely be quicker to find his way back than go on towards unknown territory. He was a boy of the lake and the shore. Deep, tangled trees in woods were not what he was used to.

Then, there was Firecrest to consider.

Meanwhile, Firecrest was having his own, quite slow, but careful dragon-thoughts. "I may not always be the most helpful dragon in the world, but Goldflame and Longtail will be needing me now. But Berry and Growler need me too…" He looked at his friends, busy inspecting their track, then he looked towards the east and sniffed and sighed again.

He made his thoughtful way back to the camp just as Berry and Growler were emerging from the undergrowth. They all looked at each other. Berry's eyes met those of Firecrest. He rushed up to him and as Firecrest leant down, hugged his great neck tight. He leant back and looked at him. "We must follow the trail. I might find my family, or some other humans that know what happened to them."

Firecrest understood the meaning. He knew how useful he would be to his friend with his fire and steam-making skills. But he was heavy and lumbering on land and he wanted to swim back and look for his own family. He looked back towards the east. "I understand," said Berry. Growler didn't understand all the words, but he understood the meaning. He trotted up to his big friend and licked him round the face, more tenderly than Berry had ever seen him be. "Woofle" he whispered to Firecrest. "Ffffh" Firecrest replied, and, turning, took heavy steps towards the water, sliding into it with ease, and with a great swish of his tail, he swam easily out into the water. It wasn't

long before he was a black blob in the distance,
and then they couldn't see him at all.

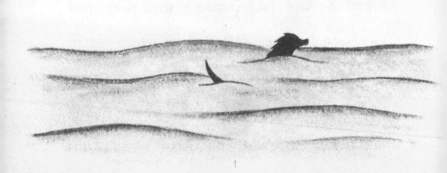

CHAPTER FOUR

TO THE RESCUE

By the time Longtail had realised she had been picked up in the air by a huge, monster wave, there was nothing she could do about it. Still lying on her back, she was riding the wave at incredible speed. As the wave tore down trees, it was so high, and she was still on top, it did little to hurt her, but she was being buffeted and banged against branches and she was very afraid. There was a roaring in her ears, and she started flailing her tail, arms and legs around hoping to catch hold of something. She seemed to be travelling for miles.

Suddenly, the wave slowed right down and FLUMP, CRASH she was down amongst trees and bushes. FLOP, she turned over and rolled onto the ground. Dazed and breathless she could hear the wave collapse itself down amongst the undergrowth, the water running around in different directions as if searching for the right way to go. She gingerly lifted herself up, licking her body where it was sore and checking herself for injuries. Battered and bruised, she looked around her and sniffed the air. "I've got a long walk home" she thought to herself. Then she snorted out a laugh. Goldflame would say, "Lazy Longtail! Get up off your big tail and get home." Although she would admit she was a lazy dragon, she was also pretty good at direction-finding. After a couple more snorts, she shook herself down, sniffed the air again, and started her trek home. She knew it would be quicker by water, but she followed the edge of it. Just for now she didn't trust it at all!

After a day of plodding along the shore, anxiously looking for somewhere that looked like home, she made a little bed of sand and settled down for the night with a big sigh.

She must have been tired, as the next thing she knew it was morning! She felt very hungry and opened her nostrils and let out some experimental blasts of steam. Yes, plenty of mosquitoes about!

She managed several mouthfuls before they gave her enough energy to nervously venture into the water. She needed to dredge up a few shrimps to give her that extra bit of energy for her long trek home.

She was just starting to get her confidence in the water when a wave nudged her in the back. It was a normal sort of wave, but it was enough to send her back to the shore. She hated being scared. How could she be a proper Dogger-dragon if she didn't like going in the water? This new, rough sea wasn't at all like her own lake and a hollow sort of ache started in her stomach. She wanted to be home! She had to be brave. She nervously waddled back in, just up to her knees. Enough to lower her head into the water and kick up a few shrimps.

Then something very strange drifted by, way out in the water, but close enough for her to hear a mewling cry. A tangle of branches and leaves...and something matted, wet, and furry frantically clinging on to it. Another "mewling" noise. She saw an upturned mouth surrounded by spiky, wet fur. "Mew-howl-owl!" It was some sort of baby fur-animal! He was in danger and being carried further out to sea! Longtail didn't have much experience of fur-animals. She liked Berry, the human-hairy animal, and his furry friend Growler, the dog, but the wild animals mostly kept their distance. She knew one thing for sure. This little fur-animal was not born to be in the water like she was. She plunged further in. The eddies and currents tugged at her, as if to remind her she was scared. She ignored them. With a few big swishes of her big powerful tail, she was soon alongside the little scrap of crying fur.

"I'm going to rescue you!" snorted Longtail with such excitement that she let out a whoosh of steam. The little wolf cub jumped back in fear. "SPLOSH" he went, into the water. Longtail was horrified! She quickly dived under the mass of branches, got under the cub, and lifted him out of the water. The cub started scrabbling around to get away but soon realised they were already halfway back to dry land. He clung on to the back of the smooth, shiny skin as best as he could, sinking his little needle teeth into Longtail's crest to get a better grip. "Ouch!". Longtail was very pleased to get back to the shore! As gently as she could, she picked the little cub up in her mouth and took him right up to the shelter of some fallen trees. She gently lay him down in the sand. The poor thing was shivering and starting to make the mewling noise again. What should she do? She had never looked after anything in her life.

"I know" she thought "Berry and Growler are the nearest thing to this little scrap than anything I know and they like WARMTH." She looked

around and spotted a useful looking tree-trunk and let out a sheet of flame. "Whoosh!" The wolf-cub jumped up, making little panicking noises. Before he could run away into the cold, Longtail had curled her long tail around him, like a cosy chair back. The little cub started to feel much better. Warmth started to seep into his shivering body and his fur started to dry out. But then he started crying again. "Hungry, hungry. HUNGRY, HUNGRY."

"Yes, all right! But what do you eat?" She looked up. A cloud of flies was dancing above some piles of wet branches "Whoosh!" She let out some steam and down they came in a tangle of insect-bodies and legs. The cub looked at them. He looked back up at Longtail. He gave her a sort of "You've got to be joking, right?" sort of a look. Longtail said "Eat, Eat!" The cub gave her a stare, then looked down at the flies. "Not food." He started making little high pitched whining noises, crying. His tummy was empty and aching.

Suddenly, a movement near the shore caught his eye. A fish flapping, caught out of the water by the waves. The wobbly little wolf cub sprung up and bounced across the sand. He sprung onto the fish and with a couple of very awkward snaps with his little teeth, swallowed it whole. He smacked his lips. "That's food. Is there more?" He started making snuffling noises with his nose as he searched around all the mess.

Longtail was worried. She was pleased the little cub at least could eat for itself, but she had no experience of fishing. Although Dogger dragons were very big, their food was just lots of very small things. They had always been very friendly with the fish and killing one on purpose would upset her. She needn't have worried. The cub was nosing his way along the shore and crunching and chomping at all sorts of things. He had just downed three or four prickly sea urchins in a row, when he suddenly looked up. A groaning and gurgling started up in his stomach. A pained look came over his face: "Bleuarhh!" - he was sick.

Longtail groaned. She was a useless dragon! It was urgent that she found the cub's family, or at least somebody who could look after him. She decided she either needed to find Berry and Growler, who would surely know, or somehow find the little cub's family. But she was a big, lumbering dragon, very slow on land, and wolves live on land, so it would be very difficult for her. While she was thinking, the little cub smacked his lips, looked at the sicked-up fish, and "Gulp!" ate it back again. He looked at the chewed-up mess of sea urchins, started to open his mouth, gave them a sniff, and left them alone. "At least he's a quick learner!" thought Longtail.

The little cub gave a satisfied lick of his lips,

had a little sit down and then looked up at Longtail. His little baby eyes started to clear. He stared at Longtail and started to focus. Then he tilted his head to one side, as if to get a better view, then tilted it to the other side. He let out a little "Yip." Then, a few more: "Yip! Yip!" It was as if he recognised Longtail!

"We've never met before!" snorted Longtail. "Who do you think I am?"

Again, the wolf cub's head tilted to one side "Squeee, squeee!" he yowled. A perfect imitation of Whistler. WHISTLER! Her long-lost baby brother! "You know Whistler? How can you? How is that possible? Where is he?"

"Squeee! Squeee!" the little cub jumped up

and down, circling round, leaping about and then running towards the trees and back again. He kept doing it. "Follow me, follow me! I know where another one of your kind is. Follow me, follow me!"

Longtail had never tried to talk to a wolf before, but what this little scrap of fur was trying to tell her was as plain as day. Or was she just imagining it? Perhaps the little cub was just being excited? Shouldn't she be concentrating on getting him back to his pack? "FOLLOW ME!" The cub started barking and making more "yipping" noises. "Come on, come on!" Longtail still wasn't sure.

The cub got quite impatient and started

barking very loudly. He was making SUCH a racket, suddenly, from a very long way away... distant howls. Wolf howls! "Awooool!" The cub sat back on its haunches, pointed his nose to the sky and broke into a proper, grown-up, if somewhat wobbly, wolf-howl, as loud as he could: "Yip, yip, YIP, YIP AWOOOOOLL!"

A chorus of delighted howls replied, "Awoooool!!!", still a long way away. The cub was so excited! So was Longtail! She let out a load of steam-snorts and bounced up and down with the cub, trying very hard not to land on him.

It took a while for the pack to reach them. Then there was a rushing sound coming from the undergrowth, and there sprang out three adult wolves, closely followed by three cubs. Eyes bright, tongues out, panting hard. They bounded up to the little cub round and round him, licking and licking him. One, a female, sicked-up some food that she had been saving in her stomach, just for him. "Proper food!" yelped the cub and downed it all in one go. He had his mum and his family back. Just as Longtail was starting to feel left out, all the cubs, including hers, bounded up to her, and started licking her too, and wagging their tails.

The adults looked on. They were so happy and grateful to Longtail, and they knew just how they could repay her. They started circling, just as the cub had done, and pointing back into the trees. "Follow us." The trouble was, Longtail was a good swimmer, but on land, she was a big lumbering, slow sort of an animal. With trees and tangled brambles, well this was going to be so difficult. How far would she have to go?

"Squeee!" said the cub again. Yes, that was Whistler's call alright. If she could find Whistler! How happy they would all be! She thought of Firecrest and how sad he had become since Whistler and Steamer had disappeared. She would give anything to see Firecrest happy again, and she had to admit she had missed little Whistler too. She sprung up and followed the wolves, who turned into the woods and off they all went.

CHAPTER FIVE

ALONE AT THE DEN

After the wave had gone, Goldflame found herself on her back, with the den, and what seemed like half of the forest, on top of her. Everything was dripping in water. With a lot of pushing and shoving, she heaved herself out from under the tangle of what had once been a lovely, cosy den.

She looked towards where she thought Longtail had been. There was nobody there. There was no shore, it was all water, which had drowned out all the familiar trees and undergrowth. She called. She took in a deep breath and shouted more loudly: "Longtail!" A horrible feeling nagged at her tummy. She tried not to panic. She took the biggest breath she could and let out a huge stream of steam: "LONGTAIL!" The steam signal echoed around the huge expanse of water. No reply. She stood up on her back legs, eyes narrowing to focus. She looked carefully around the new horizon. Water everywhere, branches and grasses ripped out of the ground and floating about on the water. But no steam signals. No Longtail. Was she a good enough swimmer to ride out a thundering wave? She let out a gasp. What about Firecrest, out at sea?

She tried again: "LONGTAIL, FIRECREST!"

She looked. She listened. Just the whispering of fallen trees as their leaves flapped about in the breeze. Goldflame sank to her knees. Her lovely gold crest fell down and draped over her back like an old scarf. A sob rose in her throat. But almost as soon as it had, she sat upright, took a deep breath, and thought: "They are both strong swimmers. They can do this. Wherever they are, they will find their way back home to me, and I don't want them to see their mother sitting here looking scared and sorry for herself."

She decided the best thing to do was to keep busy. She turned round and waded through the water until she found a slope and dry land. "I'll make another cosy den right here, for when they come home," she thought, and was soon dragging branches and gathering leaves. It kept her busy, and she needed to keep busy.

CHAPTER SIX

TRACKS AND SIGNS

Berry and Growler had followed the stream
for many hours before they decided to stop
for the night. Berry's heart had felt heavy as
he had picked his way
along, searching for clues.
He hadn't found anything. It
was only Growler's excited

sniffing that kept him going. He would have preferred to make a fire, but it was almost dark before he had made a shelter and it wasn't too cold. It was pitch black, no light at all. Berry was used to the open, where he could see the moon or stars. The trees seemed to be crowding in on him. After last night, he felt uneasy. He told himself to relax. After all, he had Growler to keep him warm, to listen and sniff out trouble, and enough fish and berries to eat. He made a bed of twigs and cosy moss, and they snuggled up for the night.

In the end, they slept well. Growler had been making little "yipping" noises in his sleep, having dog-type dreams. Berry had also been dreaming.

He was with his mother and father and very young, but big enough to help his mother collect shellfish and seaweed on a trip to the sea to go fishing. His dad was out in a little boat, trawling with his net, just as Berry himself had been only a few short days ago. His mum was collecting little seashells "I'm going to make myself a necklace" she said. "If you can help me, and we collect enough, I'll make you a bracelet too." Berry woke up with a start. Tears sprung into his eyes. Was that a made-up dream or a long-forgotten memory? Growler sat up as soon as he realised Berry was awake. He shook himself down, gave himself a few licks to feel clean for the day, and nudged Berry and gave him a little lick too. He knew that this adventure was important to Berry. He missed his home with all the usual sniffs but would stay with Berry and help him find his "shell-people". Berry was anxious to get going, so didn't take long having a bite of dried fish and some water for his breakfast. Then they were off.

Berry followed Growler all morning and was starting to feel that they were just following an animal trail. Then, suddenly, Growler got quite excited. He started wagging his tail, made a big snorting/snuffling noise and pushed through a very narrow path in the undergrowth. Soon the trees were thinning, and they were in a clearing. There, in the middle of the open space, was the remains of a campfire! Berry rushed up to it.

So did Growler, but he was after any food that might have been left behind!

Berry searched around. The ash and bits of logs in the middle of the fire were cold, and plants had started to grow out of them. There were remains of animal bones left in the soil nearby, which meant that there had been a meal. There were even the remains of an old shelter.

He saw something hard, dark, and shiny near the ashes. He rubbed it clean with his fingers. It was an old fire-flint! That might be very useful. He pushed it into his leather pouch. Even though it was obviously left behind, he felt guilty picking it up, like he was stealing.

He sat back on a log and looked around. It

didn't look like any people had been there for a while. Who were they? Were they on a hunting party? Did they live nearby? He decided to stop for the night. He would clear the fire pit and make a new fire and repair the shelter. If some people were close by, perhaps somebody would see the smoke from the fire.

He got busy collecting firewood. There were plenty of branches and twigs around and even some silver birch trees which were very useful. He had only to peel some of the thin bark off and make a little pile of shavings which would catch light easily to start the fire. He also found another flint! It wasn't such a good shape as the first one but good enough to strike with the other one. He soon made a spark, and, with a few gentle puffs against the birch bark, it burst into flames, and he soon had a proper fire.

There was no need to cook anything as Berry had been collecting more seeds and berries as they went along, and he still had plenty of cooked fish for them both to eat. He would have to start looking for more food soon, though. He was just thinking about this when he decided to skirt around the clearing and pick up a few branches and twigs to add to the fire for the night. He bent down over some twigs which were on a bare patch of earth. He stopped short, hand out about to pick them up. He stared.

They were arranged in the shape of an arrow!

An arrow that pointed into the undergrowth but which he could now see had a very narrow trail pushed through it. A sign! To follow! But who was it meant for? If only he had spotted it earlier!

He gently bent down to touch the twigs, as if

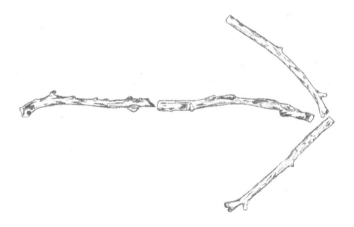

he could somehow make contact with whoever had arranged them. It was already starting to get dark, so it was impossible to do anything now.

He left the arrow there, and quickly patched up his small shelter with branches, leaves and moss and settled down for the night. Growler had already gone to sleep by the fire, but it took Berry much longer.

Why were these people on the move? Where were they going? Would his parents be with them? Or would they be nothing to do with him at all and be unfriendly? These questions were going round and round in his head until he finally dropped off to sleep.

CHAPTER SEVEN

BIG SURPRISES

Firecrest had never swum so far in the sea before. All the water that had come along with the huge wave had changed the way the land looked and turned the forest into seaside. There seemed to be more sea and more coast, as if their lovely Doggerland had somehow turned into an island. He thought a few times about whether to swim to the shore and make his way to a river to find the lake, but in the end thought it easier, for a good swimmer like him, just to keep swimming in the general direction of home and keep land in sight. Every time he found the mouth of a river entering the sea, he started to get hopeful. He would turn over and gaze under the water, looking for his seahorse friends. But all the underwater world had changed too. Instead of clear water with floating fronds of weeds and kind-faced seahorses bobbing up and down amongst them, it was all churned up, grey and cloudy.

He started to feel very nervous. Where was home? None of the trees or hills on land looked familiar. Where they lived was very flat. Night-time came and he found a safe-looking beach and made a nest for the night. He couldn't sleep, in spite of being so tired, so he looked up at the sky. It was a lovely starry night, and he knew all the stars and the shapes they made in the sky. They felt like old friends and were comforting. There was one pattern that had always looked to him like a dragon, and he always felt safe when he saw it. There it was up there now. It also told him which way was north and so he knew he was going the right way home if he kept it to his left. He gazed up at the stars for a bit longer. Every now and then a fluffy white cloud would go by, lit up by the moon. He closed his eyes and was soon fast asleep.

He woke up just after sunrise and was soon catching flies for his breakfast and keen to get on. Back in the water he carried on swimming

towards the east, keeping the coastline close-by. He stopped from time to time to turn over and look underwater. Still no seahorses. There were plenty of shellfish and starfish and a lot more rocks than his old hunting grounds. As he rolled over, something very strange caught his eye.

A huge, black blob of something, far out to sea. It looked like it was moving! Yes, it was getting bigger. Whatever it was, it seemed to be coming towards him! If it was an animal, it must be a monster! A dangerous monster? He thought it would be wise to try and find out now, while it was still a good distance away. He stood up in the water, doing his best "dragon-paddle" to stay upright, and let out a stream of steam:

"Hello! My name is Firecrest. Is there somebody there?" He waited a few moments, half-hoping he wouldn't get a reply.

A HUGE stream of steam AND FLAMES, appeared from the top of the blob, which was getting bigger by the second: "HELLOOOO! I'M BOOMER! I'M A GIANT DRAGON FROM THE NORTHLANDS!" he boomed.

BOOMER

"A giant dragon? I've never heard of one of those before." shouted Firecrest.

"HANG ON A MINUTE, I'LL COME OVER," boomed Boomer.

The blob got bigger and bigger. As soon as he was close enough to Firecrest he raised his head and blasted out a greeting: "HELLO, NICE TO MEET YOU!"

"And you!" gasped Firecrest. What a huge, amazing-looking dragon! He was dark midnight-blue on top, with a wavy crest on his back. He had white stars on his back instead of spots. His throat and tummy were bright orange with black spots. Firecrest stared. He just couldn't help it!

"Is something wrong?" boomed Boomer (a

little quieter now they were closer together).

"No! Sorry, I didn't mean to be rude. It's just that I've never seen a dragon so big and with such amazing colours."

He wondered if that was a bit rude and was about to apologise when Boomer said "Ah, you must be a Dogger dragon. I've heard stories about them but never seen one before. I had heard you were green, and I love the orange crest."

"Oh, it's just me that has the orange crest" said Firecrest, (a bit embarrassed as nobody had ever complimented him on his looks before). "But my Mum has a yellow crest, so I think that's where I get it from." Mentioning his mother suddenly made his heart sink. How was she? How was

Longtail? Had they been safe from the wave? Would they be worrying about him?

"What's the matter? Why are you out here so far from home?" asked Boomer.

Firecrest told him his story, that he had to leave his friends so he could find his way back home, and that he was worried about his mother and sister.

"That's terrible," said Boomer. "I'm out at sea because we had a violent storm. The whole ground seemed to move and shake. It was so loud, with a rumbling and roaring, and a part of our cliff fell into the sea. It seemed to push the water everywhere in great waves, even flooding where it used to be land. I was just cruising around exploring the new sea, and to see what I could find. And look! I've found a Dogger dragon!" He smiled kindly at Firecrest. "Can I help? I can swim a lot further out to sea than you, and a lot more quickly. I'll shout out if I see anything interesting."

"That would be amazing. Thank you," said Firecrest, pleased that he wasn't on his own anymore.

"RIGHT. LET'S GO!" boomed Boomer, very loudly, as he was so excited.

Boomer surged through the water and further out to sea, while Firecrest swam close to shore. Still nothing looked familiar. In fact, the coastline was getting rocky, with cliffs and even craters,

that looked like long-dead volcanoes. Firecrest
had never seen anything like it. He felt he'd
never get home. Not only that, but he was tired.
It was very difficult keeping up with Boomer!

Suddenly, everything changed…

"WHAT'S THAT?" Boomer boomed, his
voice echoing off the rocks. He powered back
through the waves, towards a grey, rocky crater,
that was sticking up out of the shore next to
the cliffs. There were faint puffs of steam
coming out of the top. Firecrest, a bit puffed,
caught up with him.

"I've heard of volcanoes" said Boomer "but
the only active ones are much further north than
even us in the Northlands. This shouldn't be

steaming. Perhaps it's waking up!"

"Is it dangerous?" asked Firecrest.

Before Boomer could give his opinion, something very amazing happened. The steam suddenly got stronger, louder, and started to speak!

"Is somebody there? Hallo? Are you there? Can you help? My name is Steamer and I've been trapped in here for years."

"STEAMER! DAD!" shouted Firecrest.

"STEAMER! DAD!" echoed Boomer. What an adventure he was having!

"Dad, is that really you?"

"Yes, it's me, it's Steamer! Who is that? Is it Firecrest?"

"Yes Dad, it's me, Firecrest! What are you doing there? It's been years! Are you trapped?"

"Yes, I'm stuck here!" shouted Steamer, from deep inside the crater.

"I'm alright now, but that storm years ago pushed the waves so high they dropped me in this place and the sides are so steep I can't get out. It's been so long. I nearly gave up hope of anybody finding me. Are you alright? Did Whistler come home? Is Goldflame alright?"

"Oh, Dad. I'm so sorry. We never did find Whistler. The rest of us are fine, although Mum is very quiet without you, and I have missed you such a lot."

There was a sob from the other side of the

rock wall. "Oh, little Whistler!"

"Anyway" said Firecrest briskly, trying not to get upset. "Let's see what we can do from this side to get you out."

"We? Who is with you?"

"ME!" boomed Boomer. "DON'T WORRY ABOUT A THING. "I'M SURE I CAN BLAST YOU OUT. STAND BACK!"

"Hold on a min…" started Steamer, hoping to get back a bit from the blast. Too late!

"WHOOOOOSH!" blasted Boomer. Flames, steam, and a big roaring. The rocks scattered everywhere, Firecrest scrambled out of the way, and the water behind the wall of rock, with Steamer in it, came rushing and tumbling out of the rocky crater. Over and over Steamer tumbled until he was floating in the sea. All went quiet.

"I hope I didn't overdo it," Boomer mumbled, apologetically, hand over his mouth.

Firecrest dared not move for a moment, with smoking, charred rocks all around him. His father lay still on his back in the water. He clambered towards him.

As he got nearer, he saw a huge smile come over Steamer's face and he let out a stream of steam in relief. "Out at last! How wonderful! My dear Firecrest. My dear new friend." He rolled over and looked at Boomer, shaking himself down, a bit battered and bruised. "My most amazing new friend!" he steamed (and stared!).

"I KNOW!" boomed Boomer "YOU'RE GOING TO SAY YOU'VE NEVER SEEN A DRAGON LIKE ME BEFORE!"

"I've always known we had giant cousins living far away" said Steamer "But I've never met one until now. How wonderful that you came to help."

"You can thank Firecrest for that," said Boomer. "He was trying to find his way back home. If he hadn't called out to me, we might never have spotted you."

Firecrest went quiet for a few moments. In his excitement at finding Steamer, he had forgotten about Goldflame and Longtail, and had not thought of Whistler.

"What do you want to do next, Firecrest?" asked his father.

"Well, I don't think Longtail would have been washed this way, and if you never saw or heard Whistler in all this time, I think we should go back to Goldflame."

His dad looked pleased. His heart had ached for Goldflame and he had never stopped worrying about her while he was trapped in the crater.

"I'M COMING TOO! THIS IS A GREAT ADVENTURE!" boomed Boomer.

So, they turned their backs on the place that had been a prison for Steamer for so long, and, with Boomer in front (even though he didn't really know where they were going) they swam back home. Firecrest thought he had never been so happy.

CHAPTER EIGHT

WOLF LAKE

Longtail was getting very tired. The wolves had stopped for the night but only to give her time to sleep. They seemed to be full of energy. They bounded on ahead of her, yipping and yapping, sniffing and snuffling. She was so much heavier than them and not suited to scrambling around in woods. Every now and then they stopped, and the wolves pretended they needed a rest just so that she could catch her breath. She knew they weren't really tired because, as soon as they stopped, the cubs all started playing with each other again, they were so pleased to be back together.

They eventually came across the banks of a river, and Longtail sploshed into it with relief. The wolves ran alongside as they all followed it down to where it opened out into a small lake.

There, in the middle of the lake surrounded by trees, and lit up by low sunshine on grey water, was a Dogger dragon, floating about and every now and then sending up a stream of steam to catch flies.

"WHISTLER!" steamed Longtail, at the top of her voice.

Whistler, who was now almost a fully grown dragon, turned over in the water with a

big splash. "What? What? LONGTAIL!" He couldn't believe his eyes.

There was Longtail surrounded by Whistler's wolf family, who were starting to bark and howl with excitement from the shores of the lake. Longtail plunged into the water, sending a huge splash which covered the wolves. They shook themselves, wagging their tails in delight. Whistler swam towards Longtail as Longtail raced through the water towards him. They crashed into each other, laughing, and steaming and Whistler shouted out his high-pitched "Squeee!" just like he used to when he was little. In fact, he went "Squeee" so many times the wolves thought their ears would explode!

Whistler and Longtail did neck and tail hugs, went round and round in the water together and nearly tied themselves in knots! At last, they calmed down and made it to the shore, where the wolf cubs danced about them, and over the top of them. There was steaming, squealing, yipping, yapping and barking!

As the light began to fall, and everyone started to settle for the night, Whistler told Longtail all he knew about what happened to him.

"I should never have run out," he said. "The storm had frightened me. The thunder and lightning were so loud. By the time I calmed down the rain was so heavy and huge waves were knocking me over. I tried calling. I couldn't make steam. I was too frightened and then it was too dark. I was completely lost. In the end I felt a tugging round my neck and a big mother wolf was dragging me out of the water. I had fallen asleep, and she thought I was drowning. I owe her my life."

He looked across at the wolves and the mother looked up towards him, her gold eyes kind and caring.

"They knew that dragons need lakes and as they lived next to this one, they carried me here. I was too small to try and get home on my own. I didn't know where I was. Actually, I still don't know where I am!" he said with a sniff. "Just that this has been my home for years and the wolves have kept me company."

"Did you ever hear Steamer calling for you?" asked Longtail.

"No".

Longtail told him the story and Whistler hung his head down low. "I'm so sorry."

A big tear ran down his face.

"Dad would still be here if it wasn't for me being a coward."

"You were a baby, it wasn't your fault," whispered Longtail. They lent against each other's necks and were quiet for a bit, and then fell asleep. Whistler realised how lonely he had been without the comforting weight of a Dogger dragon to lean against at night.

The next morning was all smiles and tears. Whistler was going home! But he would miss his adopted fur-family. They pranced around both dragons as they all made their long, difficult journey back to the spot where Longtail had rescued the little cub. After much licking from the wolves Whistler at last pushed off into the new, rough sea with Longtail, who swam with new confidence now she had her not-so-little brother by her side. They would swim until they saw land they recognised, then make their way home.

The wolves all stood in a row by the shore, large ones and small, until they couldn't sniff their large foster-brother anymore. They turned and pranced back into the woods.

CHAPTER NINE

A BIG DECISION

Berry was up bright and early. He kicked dust into the fire to put it out. He was tempted to leave it smouldering in case somebody saw it, but he knew how dangerous that could be in case it woke up and set the trees alight.

Soon he and Growler were following the arrow into the tiny track. It didn't take long before the path started to get quite steep, and they were climbing a hill. This was all new to Berry as he had lived in flatlands all his life. Even for someone so fit, he was starting to feel a bit out of breath! Soon there was more sunshine up ahead and the trees were clearing, and they came across a rocky stream that was bubbling out of the top of a hill. He rushed to the water, bent down, and cupped his hands and had a lovely drink of cold water.

As he lifted his head, and stood up, he almost cried out at the sight of another arrow, this time carved into the rock and pointing to the top of the hill. He rushed to the top, and, as he looked down the other side, what he saw nearly took his breath away. From where he stood, there was a steep slope, with the narrow track running through bushes, then grasses, and finally down to an open beach and the sea beyond.

On the beach, there were shelters. Human shelters! Just like his, but bigger and better made. He could see all sorts of signs of many people living there. Old fire pits, a small dug-out boat left near the water, a lot of piles of wood and branches heaped up. But no people. "Come on, Growler!" he shouted.

They both ran down the slope, almost tripping on long grass and brambles that were growing across the track. He wasn't used to running down slopes and soon realised he was going too fast and out of control. He grabbed at a young tree branch as he was speeding along, span round and fell over, flat into some prickly undergrowth. Bruised, and a bit embarrassed, he picked himself up and brushed the grit off his knees. He needn't have worried. All was quiet. There was nobody around to see him fall over. Growler had his mouth open, panting and wagging his tail. He liked this game!

"Hello? Hello?" Berry called. "Is anybody here?" he wandered around the huts which, on close inspection, looked abandoned. There were a few belongings, like cooking pots, and some animal skins which looked like bed covers. But the whole place felt like the people had packed up and gone somewhere.

He saw something hanging up by the entrance to one hut, just gently swinging in the breeze, as if it was waving to him. He walked up to it, and almost felt he was in a dream, like slow-motion. Hanging there. A cowrie-shell necklace. He reached up and drew the necklace through his fingers, feeling each shell. He held his breath.

He looked inside the shelter, but there was no-one there. The necklace was like a message "Yes, Berry. We were here."

Growler was busy discovering interesting things too. He had been digging and sniffing and smelt dogs! Not only that, but he also found a store of old wild boar bones, half buried in a dog-food larder near one of the huts. He sniffed excitedly. Dogs had been living with the humans! None of the dog scents were new, and they all led to the beach. The dogs had gone with the humans!

There were dragging marks in the soft soil, heading towards the water. Any footprints (or pawmarks) had been washed away. Berry followed them. Nearer the shore there were signs of boat-building. Remains of carved out tree trunks, shreds of twine made into ropes, fishing nets, all sorts. The drag marks near the water were still very clear, almost as if it hadn't been that long since whoever had gone, had dragged the boats into the water. The marks were deep, as if the boats had been heavy and built to take a lot of people, or a lot of possessions, or both. Walking along the shore, Berry thought there had been four big boats.

But then another thought struck him. This land had never been next to the sea. In his short time with his parents, there had never been any talk of Doggerland being an island. The river by the lake had gone to the sea but as far as he knew the land on this side just went on and on. This sea shouldn't be here! He looked about. Yes, he could see signs of old huts in the shallow water. There were wooden posts in lines sticking out of the mud. All the storms and floods had drowned out the settlement here. People had decided to move on. He screwed his eyes up again towards the horizon. Nothing. Just sea. Or…wait a minute! What was that dark line on the horizon? It was so thin he hadn't spotted it before. Is that land? They must have been going SOMEWHERE! He called Growler, who appeared with an old bone in his mouth. "Back up the hill!" cried Berry.

He ran and scrambled as fast as he could. Growler loved a run, but he couldn't work out why they were running away from the place that had stores of tasty bones. They finally got back to the top. Out of breath, Berry swung round and looked again out to sea. When he had been here the first time, he had been looking downwards at the settlement. Now he looked up, round the corner further out to sea. He gasped. Yes, there it was, far away on the horizon, a slither of land. He hadn't been able to see it from the huts. He could even make out distant hills and cliffs. That's where they have gone. They were searching for somewhere safer to live.

His stomach suddenly felt empty and achy, and he sank to his knees. Growler nudged him with his great hairy nose and gave him some licks. Berry had never felt like this before. When he had been washed away all those years ago, the dragons had saved him, and they made sure they put him where his old home had been and where he could live safely. They had always kept an eye on him. Then he had Growler, and he had always assumed that his family had either given him up for dead or died themselves. He had been too young then to go and explore and try and look for them. As the years went by, he had never seen any sign, no smoke, nothing to show other humans were about. He had settled down and been happy. That was then. Now what?

He sat for some time just looking at the sea. It started to get dark, and Growler gave him a nudge. "Let's get some shelter", said Berry. With heavy legs and heart, he made his way back down the slope. Of course, he knew which shelter to pick for the night. The one with the necklace. There were enough old hides and even an old, raised bed to settle in for the night. He went outside and scraped away at an old fire pit and scrambled around for some sticks and logs. There was still plenty of firewood around and about and he soon had a fire burning. He had very little food left. He shared the last of his dried fish with Growler. He would have to look for some more food in the morning before deciding what to do next. He hugged Growler close that night.

Berry woke up the next morning with a plan. There was one, small dug-out boat left on the shore. Why it had been left behind, he didn't know. Perhaps it was left in case somebody else wanted to follow? The yearning to find his family had grown strong. He went down to inspect the little boat. It had two wooden oars and even a fishing net inside.

As he was checking out to see what else was inside, he caught his breath. There, as clear as day, scratched along the side of the boat in the wood, a big straight arrow. Pointing towards the sea. "This way!" it seemed to say. Was it a message to him? Just in case he had survived all those years ago? He looked across the water. The waves were high and rough, and a small boat might not be good enough for a long journey. "That's why they made big boats" he thought.

They would have had four or more people rowing. Can I do this on my own?" He decided he had to try.

The first thing to do was to spend the day collecting food and water, enough to keep him and Growler going for some days. The net might be good to catch fish as they went along. He spent all that day hunting and gathering food.

It took all day to get enough food prepared and to pack the boat with useful things that had been left behind. He had animal skins for covers and blankets, nets, ropes, he even found a flint-headed spear. He had never hunted bigger animals for food, but perhaps now he was growing up, this spear would help him to try. He tucked everything into the boat and settled down to sleep. If it wasn't too rough in the morning, he would head straight out, in a straight line across the water and find his family.

The next morning started with a calm sea. It was the right time to go. Berry stood on the shore, with his dog by his side, and thought about the life he was leaving behind. He felt sad he hadn't been able to tell the dragons, and he hoped Firecrest had got back home safely. "Are you ready, Growler?" "Woof!" said Growler, and jumped into the boat. Berry pushed the boat off, and away they went. Pointing towards the west and the distant horizon.

CHAPTER TEN

DRAGONS!

If you had been near the dragon's den and seen all the steam and flame you would have thought there had been a terrible fire and something really bad had happened.

Goldflame's morning had started very quietly. She had finished making the new den and had nothing else left to do. She was lying in the now peaceful water of the lake, breathing little bits of steam into the air, and catching mosquitoes. Not for the first time, she was telling herself not to worry, and that they would all be back safely soon.

She didn't expect to hear a sudden BOOM!

First, she heard the most enormous rush of steam, and then: "IS THAT YOUR GOLDFLAME? IS THAT YOUR MUM?" boomed Boomer.

Goldflame jumped and sat up in the water. There, coming towards her, was the biggest, noisiest, dragon she had seen in her entire life. But she quickly forgot him. On one side of him, swam Firecrest. On the other... Steamer! Her wonderful Steamer!

Boomer and Firecrest hung back while Steamer powered through the water to join his beloved Goldflame. The splashing and steaming and tail and neck hugging!

The group had just made it back to the shore when they heard: "SQUEEE! SQUEEE!".

Out of the trees burst Longtail, with WHISTLER by her side. "SQUEEEEEEEE!". Whistler thought his chest would burst. It was the longest, loudest "squeee" of steam he had ever made. He never thought he could be so happy. He rushed towards his family.

And that's where we leave them all. For now.

ESCAPE FROM DOGGERLAND!

In *Escape from Doggerland* we find Berry and Growler facing hazards they should only face in nightmares. A close encounter with a sabre-toothed cat, bullies who want Berry's boat, and the legend of a fierce monster.

On Doggerland, the dragons have big decisions to make, as their world slowly disappears under the sea. Can they adapt? Or should they leave? Having only just found each other, loyalties are stretched to the limit as they face having to go their separate ways.

"I really enjoyed the story and didn't want it to end, I'm curious as to what happened next to all the characters".

Amber, aged 9

Confident readers from the age of 6+ will love *Dragons of Doggerland*.

The author is anxious not to put too much emphasis on actual chronological ages, having been an advanced reader herself, aged 4!

N
E
W
S

THE BIG WAVE

SEAHORSES HOME

OLD VOLCANO

SHALLOW LANDS AND MARSHES

140

DOGGERLAND

DOGGER BANK HILL

DRAGONS'
DEN

G LAKE

BERRY'S
HOME

WOLF
LAKE

SHALLOW LANDS
AND MARSHES